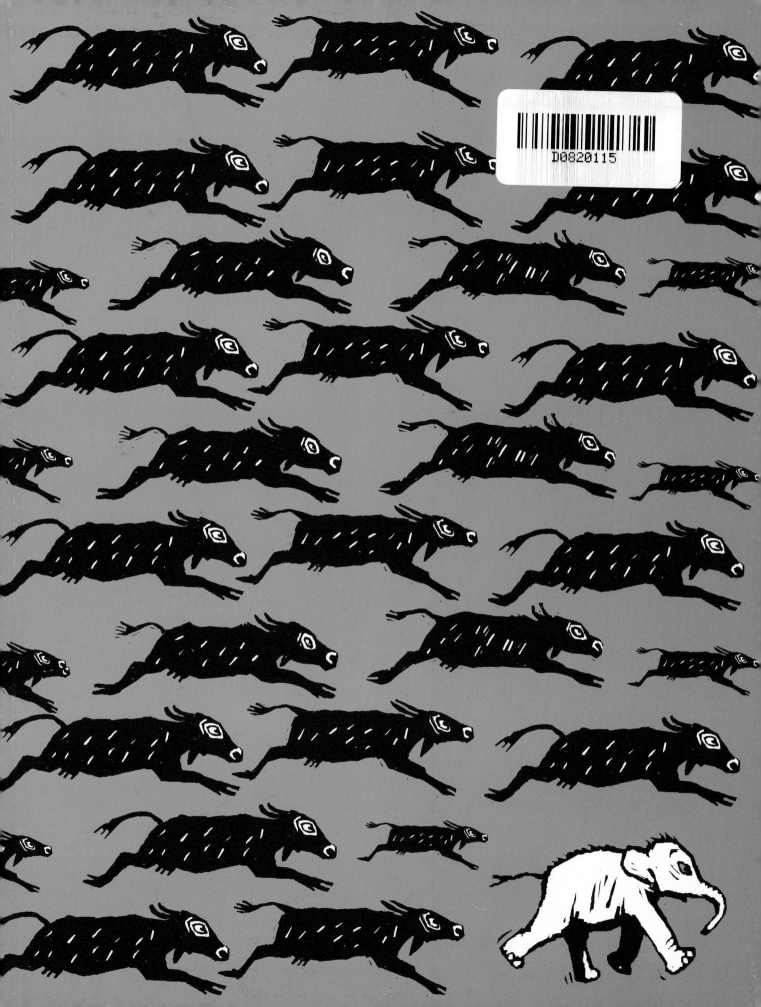

Elephants never forget!

by Anushka Ravishankar

illustrated by Christiane Pieper

It was quiet in the jungle   When a sudden storm came.

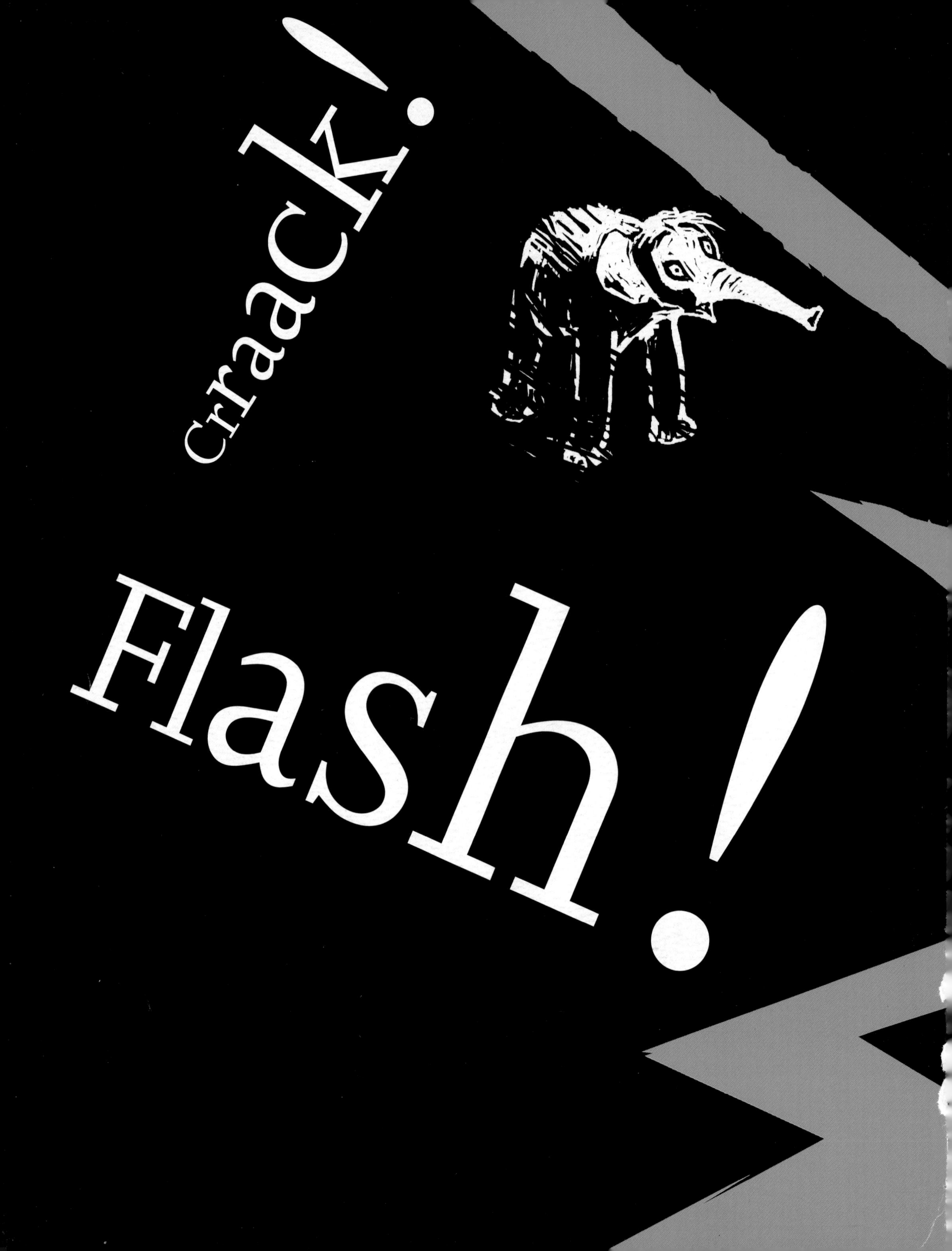
Crraack!
Flash!

BOOM!

There was thunder, lightning, rain!

TOOT! TOOT!
The elephant
Trumpeted in fright.

HOOT! HOOT! HOOT!

The wind replied.

When the rain stopped
And the sun shone,

The elephant found

He was all alone.

Splatter!

Splitter!

Chitter!

Chatter!

He heard a bunch of monkeys natter.

They pushed and they pulled,
They slid and they swung,
They rocked and they rode—
They threw and they flung!

Squish!
Splosh!
Blish!
Blosh!

CCrrraCk!

A coconut hit him on the head.

Enough, thought the elephant,
And he fled.

He needed some water
To wash himself clean.

The buffaloes looked so calm, so serene.

The water was lovely, cool and green.

The elephant thought
He could stay with them!

Maybe even play with them?

With a buffalo calf
He tumbled and wallowed.

BELLOW!

The buffalo led
And the elephant followed.

The elephant felt he had found a friend.

Their frolicking came to an end.

The buffaloes were leaving!
The elephant was sad.

Why didn't they like him?
Was he rude? Was he bad?

The reason they'd run
was suddenly clear . . .

R O A

The elephant trembled in fear.

BELLLLOOOOO

OW!

He could not move, he was terrified.
A buffalo pushed him aside.

As the herd ran away, it took him along.

He stayed on with them.
He grew big and strong.

The elephant cleared the buffaloes' path.

He helped them take a shower bath.

He found them leaves when the grass was dry.

Now the tiger didn't dare come by!

His ears were too large,
His nose was too long,

His shape was quite odd,
And his color all wrong.

He could only trumpet, not bellow, and yet
He liked being a buffalo, muddy and wet.

As they lazily basked by the river one day . . .

Some thirsty elephants
came that way.

The buffaloes decided
they'd rather not stay.

T! TOOOoT!

The elephants called.

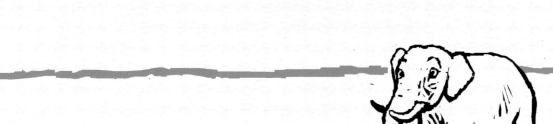

Belloow! Belloooow!

The buffaloes bawled.

Here?

        Or there?

Where should he go?

An elephant?

        Or a buffalo?

In the end, the answer was plain—

A buffalo he would always remain!

Originally published by Tara Publishing, Chennai, India
(www.tarabooks.com).

www.houghtonmifflinbooks.com

The text of this book is set in Joanna.
The illustrations are digitally created.

Library of Congress Cataloging-in-Publication Data

Ravishankar, Anushka.
  Elephants never forget / written by Anushka Ravishankar ;
illustrated by Christiane Pieper.
     p. cm.
  Summary: A lonely elephant meets a herd of buffaloes and decides
to stay with them, but when they meet up with some elephants, he
must make an important decision.
  ISBN-13: 978-0-618-99784-8
  [1. Elephants—Fiction. 2. Buffaloes—Fiction. 3. Identity—Fiction.
4. Stories in rhyme.] I. Pieper, Christiane, ill. II. Title.
  PZ8.3.R2325El 2008
  [E]—dc22
                                    2007025745

Printed in Singapore

TWP 10 9 8 7 6 5 4 3 2 1